Box-Office Smash

THE OPPORTUNITY

Box-Office Smash

D. M. PAIGE

darbycreek

MINNEAPOLIS

Text copyright © 2013 by Lerner Publishing Group, Inc.

Darby Creek
A division of Lerner Publishing Group, Inc.
241 First Avenue North
Minneapolis, MN 55401 U.S.A.

Website address: www.lernerbooks.com

Cover and interior photographs © Felix Mizioznikov/Dreamstime.com (boy); © iStockphoto.com/Jordan McCullough (title texture).

Main body text set in Janson Text LT Std 12/17.
Typeface provided by Linotype AG.

The Cataloging-in-Publication Data for *Box-Office Smash* is on file at the Library of Congress.
    ISBN: 978–1–4677–1371–9 (LB)
    ISBN: 978–1–4677–1673–4 (EB)

Manufactured in the United States of America
1 – SB – 7/15/13

In order to succeed, your desire for success should be greater than your fear of failure.

—*Bill Cosby*

PROLOGUE

Dear Mr. Hart:

I am pleased to welcome you into the Harmon Holt internship program.

Jason, unlike the other recipients, you have a GPA well below the top ten percent. But the artistry and intelligence displayed in your videos makes you an ideal candidate for my program.

Not everyone who succeeds has a perfect GPA or a perfect record of behavior. I don't know any successful person who hasn't made mistakes along the way. For you more than anyone, this internship represents a door that you might not have found on your own. I hope you choose to walk through it.

All internship recipients will be considered for the Henry Holt Scholarship given annually to the student or students who make an extraordinary impression during their internship.

It may be hard to see it now, but the distance between me and you is hard work and opportunity. I am giving you the opportunity. The rest is up to you.

Sincerely,
Harmon Holt

ONE

I was in the cafeteria, putting the finishing touches on my project, when it happened. Trig Anderson pushed it onto the floor, and it broke into a million pieces. It was my fault for working on it in public. I wanted to get it done in time for fourth period, and now it would never be done.

Trig was a bully. He had pretty much avoided me until now, since I had my own reputation to protect me. But my project sitting out on the cafeteria table must have been too hard for him to resist.

"Oops," Trig said, when it was completely clear that everything he did was on purpose.

I leaned down to pick up the pieces, but Trig wasn't done with me yet. He kicked the box away from me.

I finally turned to face him. Ignoring him was never going to work.

"Did I break your dollies?" Trig said with an edge.

They weren't dolls. But even I could see how he would think so.

It started a few months ago. My teacher, Ms. A., taught us some simple animation called Claymation. You move these little figures a tiny bit at a time in front of a stop-motion camera. The result was really cool. My video got me my very first A.

I'd started out with a parody of those ghost movies; I'd called mine *Paranormal Inactivity*. My ghosts weren't scary; they were lazy.

I kept making the videos long after the project was over. I moved on to other genres—comedy and drama. I was good at it. Ideas kept flooding in out of nowhere. And Mrs. A was cool enough to let me do the final project using stop-motion too. I'd been uploading each video to YouTube, and I'd gotten a few hits.

Trig was twice my size. Bigger, broader—but I was faster. And the doll remark was the last straw.

I got in Trig's face. Or as close as his face as I could. I raised my fist. He laughed and pushed me against the wall. In a few short seconds, people would surround us, someone would yell "fight!" But right now it was just me and Trig.

He gave me a look that seemed to ask if I was sure I wanted to do this. Because he was definitely capable of wiping the floor with me.

Vice Principal Masters separated us suddenly, which was surprising because Masters was a good foot shorter than me and two feet shorter than Trig. But he was strong for a little guy.

Masters took Trig with him to his office but sent me to the counselor's office.

I wondered what my punishment would be. Detention. Suspension. The school had a zero-tolerance policy. But my punch never even made contact. Worse than that, I thought of the pieces of my project that were still on the floor of the cafeteria. I could put the pieces back together, but still I felt like I'd lost something I couldn't quite place. Maybe it was just that I was used to losing. I'd been doing it all my life.

TWO

"Look, Mrs. Hamilton. He started it," I began to explain as I sat down in the chair opposite her desk. The words sounded lame even though they were true. Mrs. Hamilton and I had spent a ton of time together like this. Her looking disappointed, me wondering how she could still seem so surprised that I'd screwed up.

"You're not here about that—although we do need to discuss it. We're here about this." And with that, she handed me a blue envelope with double Hs on it.

I took the envelope and turned it over in my hands.

"What's this?" I opened the letter and read it, and then I reread it. It still didn't make any sense. I read a little of it out loud. "I am pleased to welcome you into the Harmon Holt internship program."

I looked up from the paper to Mrs. Hamilton's beaming face.

"Harmon Holt wants to give me an internship on a movie set in L.A.?"

"It appears so."

"What does some rich mystery guy want with me anyway?"

"Jason, he sees what we all see . . . a whole lot of potential. I don't want to still be saying that a year from now or two years from now. I don't ever want to be saying what a waste. Either you lose it or use it."

Mrs. Hamilton's tough-love routine wasn't working on me.

"Let me guess: this is my last chance," I said bitterly. It wasn't Mrs. Hamilton's fault. It was her job to be cheerful and helpful and annoying.

"In a way, it's your first one."

I looked up at her, surprised.

"Take it, Jason."

For the first time, I was listening to what Mrs. Hamilton had to say.

THREE

I didn't have to ask Stella for permission. Stella wasn't my mom. I had to call my child services social worker, Nina. In the steady stream of foster mommas and dads, group homes, etc., Nina was the only constant. She'd been placing me since I was a baby.

I hadn't had some terrible mom. I just had a teenaged one who was too young to take care of me. And she was gone so early that I didn't even remember her. I got it. I was seventeen now, and I wasn't ready to take care of another person. I didn't think I'd ever be. It was hard enough to take care of myself.

This house wasn't a bad one. There was enough food. It was clean. There were a lot of kids. So many that I was mostly left alone— which I preferred.

When I got in from school, afternoon snacks were already being served assembly-line style in the kitchen. Stella was helping one of the little ones spread almond butter on his sandwich. He was allergic to peanut butter. Without looking, Stella knew I was there.

"Jason, you're late. Was it detention or something else?" She didn't sound judgy; she just took her mealtimes very seriously.

I wasn't ready to tell her about the internship yet. "I think I'll just head upstairs and start my homework," I said. She raised her eyebrows, like now she was really worried about me. But she handed me a plate with a sandwich on it and let me go.

"No crumbs on the bed, mister," she said and returned to supervising the sandwich line.

I shared a room with the second-oldest kid, Tim, who was sixteen. We hadn't become friends exactly. But we respected each other's space. And every once in a while Tim would show up with tiny things that he thought might work in my videos.

Tim wasn't here because he had basketball practice.

I sank down on my bed and put the plate there, too. I took a bite of the sandwich. Roast beef. And then reached in my pocket and took the letter out again.

A few minutes later, Stella called from downstairs, "Jason, visitor."

Stella was waiting at the bottom of the stairs, her arms crossed over her chest. She put a hand on my shoulder. I couldn't remember her doing that since the first time I'd met her, a year ago. She knew about the internship. She was already beginning to say good-bye, even though I didn't leave for a week.

"Nina's out on the porch. Why didn't you tell me?"

I shrugged.

"Good news like this. One of my kids being picked by Harmon Holt. Between you and Tim,

I'll have stories to have the other kids to reach up to for years."

I shrugged again. Tim was likely to get a scholarship to some college if he kept growing and kept nailing three-pointers.

"You know me, I'll probably only last a week."

"Bite your tongue, Jason Hart. Those Hollywood types have nothing on you." Her face fell as if she was thinking of something, "I'll hold your room as long as I can. I think I can have you back in the fall."

I nodded, knowing that there was a very big chance that when I got back someone else would be sleeping in my bed. Stella was a woman of her word. If she said she'd try, then she'd try, but there were no guarantees.

"We'll miss you," Stella said as I pushed my way out the front door.

Will you miss me, or my check? I thought. I reminded myself that Stella's house was the one I wanted to live out the rest of my care in. She wasn't warm and fuzzy, but she didn't yell or hit—or worse.

Nina was sitting on the porch, folder in hand. It was open, and I could see a copy of the blue letter inside.

"Please tell me that I still get to get out of here for the summer." There was still a chance that someone in child services thought that this opportunity was just an opportunity for me to get into trouble.

Nina nodded.

"I'm proud of you. This could be a great opportunity for you. Don't blow it."

"Thanks a lot," I bit back.

I sat down beside her.

"Hey, look at me," she said quietly.

I kept my eyes on the cold, hard stone steps.

"Look at me," she repeated, her voice switching to that special no-nonsense tone that made me snap to. "I know you better than almost anyone. I know that are brilliant and smart and talented. I also know that sometimes you get in your own way. Give yourself permission to be great."

I thought about making a joke about her stealing that line off a poster on Mrs. Hamilton's wall, or whether she'd been watching the Oprah channel or something. But I kept my mouth shut for once. We sat there for the longest time. She was probably hoping that her words would have time to sink in. Me, I think I was trying to adjust to the idea that for the first time in my life, Nina wasn't going to be a phone call and a short drive in her beat-up Toyota away. We would be on opposite sides of the country.

Suddenly, she handed me a small wrapped package.

Presents were not allowed between social worker and ward of the state, but Nina had made a few exceptions for birthdays and Christmas.

But it wasn't either.

"I could totally get in trouble for this. So it never happened."

"What is it?"

"It's for your trip."

I opened it. A smartphone. An iPhone like the other kids at school had, instead of my government-issued one that didn't do crap.

"It's unlimited minutes and data, so you have no excuse but to check in."

I had just turned seventeen, but we both knew what my next birthday meant. It meant that I would age out of the system and Nina would no longer be required by law to check in on me once a month. I believed that she would still check in on me.

"Thank you, Nina," I said, not just talking about the phone.

FOUR

When I landed in L.A., I was surprised to find a guy holding a card with my name on it, like I was someone famous or important or something.

"I'm Nick, one of Mr. Holt's assistants. You must be Jason Hart. Nice to meet you, man."

Nick tried to grab my bag, but I held onto it. When we got to the SUV, I couldn't help but be impressed—it was a fully tricked-out Range Rover.

"We'll take you to the home you'll be staying in."

"Home?"

"The dorms are full this summer. Too many kids taking extension courses. I know that you'll hate missing out on the dorm experience, but I think we've found something that will suit you even better."

"I think I already know how to live in small spaces," I said.

"I meant hanging with other kids doing internships," he said, completely ignoring my dig at foster-care life.

I shrugged, "Why would I want to hang out with kids I will never see again?"

He laughed. "It's not the length of time you know someone that matters. It's quality over quantity in all things. I haven't known you for long, and I feel like I already know you."

I guessed somewhere in my file it said Jason Hart "doesn't play well with others," and this guy was prepared for that. Or maybe he was just always this cool. I gave up trying to get a reaction from him.

"So, where to?" I asked as the car got moving. I was annoyed already. But I might as well get info about my summer while I could.

FIVE

We pulled into the driveway in front of a white building that seemed to stretch a whole city block.

"A hotel?" I asked.

"The Oakland Apartments. It's the place most kids stay in when they first land in L.A. for auditions. They lease by the week, and the complex is conveniently located near most of the studios. It will make your commute easier, and you'll get to know other kids who are in the biz."

Was I really a kid who was in the biz now? I couldn't wrap my head around it.

Nick kept talking. "They have tutors and acting classes and a floor with an RA for kids whose parents can't be here with them."

Walking down the halls of the Oakland was nothing like walking down the halls of any apartment building back home. Both were noisy, but that was all that they had in common. There were kids everywhere. Little kids singing at the top of their lungs. A girl about my age in full cheerleading costume dong a cartwheel right past me.

When she was right side up, she looked at me and asked, "What did you think? Would you buy me as a vampire cheerleader?"

Right side up, she was pretty. Not DC-pretty, like the girls at Clinton High. She was TV- or movie-pretty. Big brown eyes. Full, glossed lips. One of those noses that turned up at the end. Deep brown skin that seemed to be glowing, probably from her gymnastics.

I shook my head. "You're way too pretty to be a vampire."

She pouted as if I knew nothing. "All the vampires on the CW are gorgeous."

"Not as gorgeous as you."

She smiled and cartwheeled away. I almost followed, but Nick stopped me with a hand on my shoulder. I'd actually forgotten that he was still in the hallway with me.

"Let's get you unpacked, Romeo."

"You're right. I think I'm going to like it here."

SIX

Nick assured me that the RA would be by later to check on me. He gave me his business card and left me alone. The room was small, but it was the first time I'd had one all to myself.

There was a package on the table with my name on it.

I opened it. A top-of-the-line HD camera. The note inside said, "Good luck. —HH."

I turned the camera over in my hands. I'd been borrowing one from school all year. I never thought I'd have my own. There had to be a catch. All of it felt unreal somehow.

I sat down and began to figure out the camera.

I may have fallen asleep with it.

***

The Oakland actually had a car service that dropped kids at the studios in the morning. I took one to Hemingway Studios, where *The Subdivision* was being shot. It was a horror movie. But a big-budget one.

My name was on a list at the gate, but when I reached the studio door, no one was there to meet me. Everyone was busy, moving in a million different directions. It looked different than I expected. The actors stayed in trailers—which was funny because I'd thought people spent their lives trying to get out of double-wides, not into them.

The set itself was pretty awesome. It looked like a house, only with a wall missing. Cameras and lights stood where the wall should have been.

The crew was getting ready to shoot something.

I stopped one of the guys with headsets. He was really young, so I wasn't too afraid to ask him, "Hi, I'm new, I'm Jason. Where do I . . ."

The kid got on the headset and mumbled into it, "Jason's here. By the house set. Stay put, kid. He'll be right with you." Then he rushed off.

I stood by the director's chair, taking it all in. I stuck my hands in my pockets. It was weird being the only person without a purpose when everyone else had one.

A few minutes later a guy who looked like he wasn't that much older than me came and sat down in the director's chair. I'd been seeing Brent Tollin's films since I was a kid. But I had never seen what he looked like. He handed me a walkie-talkie cell phone and a headset of my own.

"Keep this on you at all times. But when we're rolling, put it on silent." He looked me in the eye when he said it, like it was really important and he thought I would forget. I shoved the phone in my back pocket. I guess he had to be pretty particular to keep something so massive running smoothly.

When he was done giving me instructions, I blurted, "Your work is really something else. When I saw *Demon Gate* . . . I didn't even know you could do that with a camera."

He began to laugh.

I stiffened. This was why I never gave compliments.

Brent was a jerk who couldn't take a compliment from an intern.

"No, man. I'm not Brent. I'm Sam. The head PA. I'm in charge of interns this summer," he said proudly.

"Then why didn't you stop me?" I demanded.

"I should have introduced myself, man. It felt good to be the big fish on set—even if it was all in your head."

"So when do I get to meet Brent?" I asked, feeling impatient. As we got further away from the cameras and the lights, things got increasingly less exciting. I wanted to stay where the action was. Not look at wardrobe, makeup, and all that.

"Maybe tomorrow. Maybe never."

I stopped walking.

"What?"

He stopped too and looked at me.

"Everyone walks in here and thinks that they're going to be the big dog on set. But we all start at the bottom. Listen, kid, it's a film set. It's controlled chaos. At some point he might yell at you because you gave him lukewarm coffee. If you're lucky."

"But I'm here to learn from him," I said, crossing my arms over my chest, feeling defensive. Like I had been the butt of some elaborate joke. I thought about Harmon Holt's letter. He sounded like he was for real. Maybe Harmon didn't hold enough weight in the in the film world. But I'd thought the Holt name held weight everywhere.

"You *are* learning from him. All of this, every little piece, from the craft services table to the guy who runs the camera, is here because of him."

"So basically the studio gets free labor just for the opportunity to be in the same studio with Brent," I snapped back. It wasn't his fault. But he was the one standing in front of me.

"Everyone feels this way at first. But once you get into the swing of it, you'll be into it again. I swear." Sam started walking and looked back at me as if to say, "Are you in or out?"

I stuck my hands in my pockets and took a few steps behind him, not committing.

"So, every week you'll be in a different department. By the end of the summer you'll know exactly how a film set works. And if you stick to this, then on every set you get to move up too. Or some people pick a department like costumes or props and stick to it. It's a grind. Better than nine-to-fiving it in an office," Sam said, smiling broader. I noticed dark circles under his eyes. He was young, but he was tired.

Where would I start? Sitting next to the director? Chauffeuring around a hot actress?

"You've going to love it," the not-director said. But the way he said it, I was almost certain that I was going to really, really hate it.

SEVEN

"You want me to do what?" I asked, looking at the table in disbelief.

There were a million different kinds of breakfast foods, from a fresh fruit salad to a tray of bagels with every topping imaginable to yogurt bars and breakfast bars. Etc. Etc. When Sam first led me to the table I'd thought , *Score, free food!* But a second later, when he explained that it was my job, my mouth stopped watering and my head started boiling.

"I'm not a waiter—" I said. I remembered the card that Nick, Harmon's assistant, had given me. Maybe if I called, they could get me a better gig. But then I'd be that kid who called for help. I couldn't do that.

Sam was on a roll, so I tuned back in.

"You are whatever we need you to be," Sam said with a smile that said he thought I had more to learn. "Suck it up, intern. It's not a bad gig. All the food you want. Wherever you work, you can pretty much check your pride at the door if you want to make it in this business."

I nodded, but I reminded myself I could still walk away. I had a return ticket to DC. Maybe I could spend a few days in L.A. before anyone reported me. It could be fun.

"Jerry is our caterer supplier. You'll meet him at lunch. He comes three times a day and brings the real food for breakfast, lunch, and dinner. You'll help him set up and clean up. Throughout the day you just make sure that the table is restocked. There's a closet in the production office where you can get anything you need. Just make sure that you always have strawberry licorice on hand—"

"Why? Because the world would end if the

table is missing strawberry licorice?"

"Something like that. Our star is obsessed with it. It's all I've ever seen her eat," he said without even an ounce of sarcasm.

My ears perked up at the mention of Becca Cody. I had seen a couple of her movies. Not in the theater, but on TV—she was good, really good. And she was hot. Really hot. The kind of girl that I would cast in a movie of my own if I was casting a real live person. And the kind of girl I would cast in my real life if I could.

Her first movie was *The Darkest House*. It was a pretty low-budget horror film that became a cult classic and put her on the map. But instead of becoming a scream queen, she'd moved on to some really heavy-duty dramatic roles, playing an Iraq vet's kid and then the lead in one of those futuristic teen dramas where only kids have survived the apocalypse. She got nominated for an Oscar for the first one, and the second one was a huge, huge box office smash.

I couldn't imagine anything I made blowing up like that. I had a few hundred hits on my videos, and it felt good to know that some people liked them. But to know the whole world was watching my every move like it did hers? I couldn't even imagine it.

Even though we were on the same set, I knew we were living in two very different worlds. Paparazzi followed her every move. People knew who she was dating and when they broke up. People knew when she went to Starbucks and when she stayed out past curfew. Her whole life was lived in front of the camera, except for when she was in her house or in this studio.

Becca was heading toward us. She was wearing one of those pink jogging suits that girls wore at school. Sometimes with words on their butts. Words like *sexy* or *juicy* that the principal decided were against dress code. They were distracting to other students or whatever.

Becca Cody approached the table. My eyes didn't know where to look. Her big, dark brown eyes, her perfect skin, her full, glossed lips, her jet-black hair pulled into a ponytail on top of her head. Her unbelievable body, whose outline I could see in the tight terrycloth. She reached for the licorice on the table.

"Is it the licorice, or are you really happy to see me?" I blurted. I smiled too broadly at her, waiting for her response.

She looked up, surprised. Maybe not used to making small talk with the help.

"Do you think that you're the first guy to try and use that line on me?" She frowned at me.

"No, but I'm the first guy who really, really meant it," I said quickly.

She laughed but then frowned again, like she'd decided she was supposed to be annoyed. But the corners of her gorgeous mouth turned up a little, meaning she was maybe a little less than annoyed.

She took the licorice and walked away.

Maybe craft services wouldn't be so bad after all.

EIGHT

The next day I didn't see her at all. I did see a lot of sweaty crewmen. A couple cute PAs. And I met a lot of other people on staff, because everyone had to eat.

Jerry, the guy in charge of the meals, didn't look like he would be in food service either. He looked like an actor. He had a square jaw and hair that didn't move.

"Actor, director, writer?" he asked when we were carrying crates of snack bars out of his catering van.

"I guess kind of all three."

I'd never actually ever been on camera, but my voice had. I told him about my videos.

"I'll check them out. Good for you, kid. Everybody comes to Hollywood with a dream. I was going to be like the next George Clooney or something. But it didn't happen. Instead, I discovered I had a knack for food."

He didn't sound bitter about his failure. He sounded happy about it. "I have ten trucks and ten guys who work for me. And a house in Bel Air and a wife who's hotter than a Kardashian. It wasn't the story that I would have written for myself. But I'm still a Hollywood success story."

"That's cool, man."

There was no real way to cop an attitude with Jerry. He was a straight shooter and a hard worker. He didn't make me lift anything he wasn't lifting himself. And he wouldn't take crap even if I was dishing it.

NINE

On the third day on set, I had gotten the hang of keeping the table stocked and was on a first-name basis with a few of the other crew members.

When I could get a break from the table, I would go and watch them tape.

I knew what Brent looked like now. He was holding court from his director's chair.

"And action," he called out.

Something in my gut tightened at the sound of the word *action*. It all felt somehow a little more real. A little of part of me spun toward the future. Me sitting in my own director's chair. Me setting a whole crew into motion with a single word. I shook it off and focused on the tiny screen that was next to the director's chair. Brent could see what the shot looked like while the cameras rolled.

Becca was on the set. She was different in front of the camera. I think more alive somehow. Like she was lit up from within—or maybe that was the effect of the lighting crew and the makeup people.

I had never seen anyone transform before. But that's what she did. For a split second I forgot about the missing wall. For a split second I felt like I was really there.

"And cut," Brent said from off camera. Becca sighed and turned into bratty teenager again. She relaxed her shoulders, slouching back into herself.

"Let's go again," he insisted.

"I thought it was perfect. I felt good about that take, Brent."

"I think you can do better." His voice was firm and challenging at the same time.

She rolled her eyes. And I was totally with her. Her take had been pretty dead-on.

"You're scared. You're alone. You're hoping that the guy of your dreams is behind that door. But you're not really sure if he's a good guy or your worst nightmare." He painted a picture with his words.

She was still frowning, but she nodded. She took a deep breath and straightened her posture. She did it again. Only this time she was better.

I saw firsthand what a good director could do. Ask for more. And actually get it.

TEN

"Today is purple," announced Sarah, the assistant script coordinator, from her position in front of the copier. Had she spent too much time with toner fumes?

"Today is Wednesday," I quipped.

She laughed, not like it was the funniest thing ever, but like she figured I deserved something for making an effort.

"The colored pages are the new pages. Every day is a different color so people don't get confused. Every person in this building gets a new script every day."

She handed me a script fresh off the copier. Bound with staples. There were more purple than white pages. There must have been a lot of changes since yesterday.

"Seems like a lot of trees have died for this film."

"I know, but we recycle."

It was my first day helping the script coordinator. He was the guy who made sure that everyone got the right copy of the script that was shooting today. And of course he had an assistant. Everybody seemed to have an assistant.

I took the heavy stack of scripts that Sarah gave me and began to make the rounds.

Now I was a delivery boy. Great. Each script had a name written on it.

When I got near the bottom of the stack, I found Becca's name. It was stupid, but my heart sped up just looking at her name written in marker. I had a good excuse to see her again.

I found her in wardrobe. She was wearing her uniform of terry sweats again. She was going through the racks of wardrobe for her next change.

"Can we do something a little less revealing?" she asked. She must have assumed I was someone else. She paused when she saw me and rolled her eyes. I guessed that she had not forgotten about the licorice thing.

I handed a script to Becca. I considered apologizing for the licorice thing. But it seemed too late now. And she seemed like the type to hold a grudge.

As she looked at the script, her eyes widened.

I headed out of the trailer. A few seconds later I heard the sound of her flip-flops catching up with me. Her hand was on my arm and she was looking at me.

"I need your help."

"Is that a line—" I came back fast, smiling and proud of myself for actually saying the right thing at the right time. I was surprised I could actually speak, because a part of her was touching a part of me.

"No, I'm serious. It's life or death."

She pulled me toward her trailer.

I wondered what life or death was for Becca Cody. It couldn't be the same as what it was back where I was from. Broken nail? Licorice shortage? I didn't really care so much, because her hand had slipped down from my arm to my hand. She was holding my hand.

ELEVEN

"So where's the fire? Or is this a food services–related emergency? Are you out of those yogurt bars?" I was talking too much, but I couldn't stop.

I was standing in Becca's trailer. Me, Jason Hart! I wanted to pull out my phone and make a video. I wanted to post it to YouTube. I wanted everyone I'd ever met to see me here.

But I clamped the scripts under my elbow and shoved my hands further into my pockets.

She sat down on her couch and motioned for me to take a seat. I sat across from her in the trailer. It wasn't like any trailer I'd ever seen. It was as if someone had pimped her trailer, like that old show on MTV where they used to pimp rides. There was a flat screen and a bed and mini fridge. There was a yoga mat set up on the floor in the corner. And one of those exercise machines where you move your legs in a circle.

"Pretty sweet setup you got here," I said with a low whistle, trying to make myself take up more space. I sat up straighter. Flexed all my muscles.

"You okay?" she asked. "You look a little . . ."

"Like I didn't belong here?" I blurted.

"I was going to say tense," she countered.

I slouched a little.

"Do you want something? Water, soda? Coffee? I just got this thing, but I don't know how to work it." She pointed to one of those fancy coffee machines sitting on top of her mini fridge.

"That's okay. Water's fine."

When she opened one of the cabinets I noticed that she had a huge stash of licorice. She didn't really have to come out of her trailer at all. Did she just want the company? Did she want to see me? She did invite me to her trailer, after all.

That had to mean something. But what?

I put down my last few scripts when she handed me a bottle of water. I opened it and took a big gulp.

Finally, I couldn't take it anymore. I needed to know.

"What am I doing here?"

"I need help with my lines, and you didn't look that busy. So I thought . . . Minnie usually helps run lines with me, but she's on set today. She has her big death scene. Anyway, I do better if someone reads with me. What do you think?"

She picked up one of the scripts and handed it to me.

"Okay," I said, but I was reeling. I'd seen her act. And she was so very good. The stuff I'd done was amateur hour.

She opened the script to her first scene. "You'll be Hallie. I'm Kara, of course."

"You want me to read the girl's part?" I asked, looking at the script in disbelief.

"Is that a problem for you?" she asked innocently.

It was kind of a problem, but I remembered

what Sam said about checking my pride at the door to get what I wanted. I didn't stand a chance with Becca, but I could at least stay in the room a little longer if I did this.

She patted the seat beside her on the tiny sofa. And I moved next to her.

I raised my voice a couple of octaves and tried the line. "What do you think you're doing with him? He's so not right for you."

She began to giggle.

I looked at her, confused.

She had her hand in front of her pretty mouth, trying to stop herself.

"You don't have to do a voice. I just need to learn my cues."

"Oh. Maybe you should just wait for Minnie." I felt the blood rushing to my face. I wasn't good at being embarrassed. I guess no one was.

"I didn't mean to offend you. Please—Jason."

She remembered my name. Becca was saying my name. And I was frozen in my tracks.

I sat back down

"From the top," she said, shaking off the laughter.

I sat back down.

"You're adorable," she blurted.

I don't think anyone had ever called me adorable. And I didn't think I would like it. But I didn't mind it so much when she said it.

We began again.

I was suddenly aware of how close we were. Even though the scene was the opposite of romantic, we were both not looking at her pages much anymore and we were looking at each other a lot. She moved away from me and reached for some of her licorice.

When we got near the end of the scene, I noticed that she'd skipped ahead a few lines.

I put my hand up like I was raising it in class and stopped her.

"You missed a line, Becca."

"No, I didn't." She looked up, her eyes flashing.

"Yes, you did."

I showed her the script. I was close enough that I could smell her perfume. I felt a little dizzy. I inhaled a mix of fresh flowers and something sweet like vanilla.

She waved the paper away.

"I don't need to see it. Just read it to me."

There was something in the way that she was not looking at the paper that hit me. But it couldn't be. She read scripts for a living. There was no way that she couldn't read.

She caught me looking at her.

She swiped the script from me and began rushing me toward the door.

"You know what, I think I've got it. Thanks so much for helping me. But I think I can take it from here."

"You can't, can you?" I asked, looking down at the paper that she was now crumpling in her hand.

"I can. I just get some of the letters mixed up sometimes. I'm dyslexic. I have a special tutor for it. But she's not here every day."

That couldn't be easy when you read scripts for a living. I felt a pang in my chest somewhere for her.

She sighed heavily. "I'm fine usually, but when I get last-minute pages like this—which doesn't happen often on Brent's films. But when it does, I totally freak."

She looked at me again. I realized that I hadn't actually said anything yet. But I wanted my words to be the right ones, and I wasn't actually good at doing that. Especially with girls. Especially with famous girls who might have just shared their biggest secret with me.

TWELVE

"Don't tell, okay?" she said. Her voice sounded shaky and fierce at the exact same time. She trained her gorgeous eyes on me, and for a split second I felt like I would do anything she asked.

"Who would I tell?" I said, not sure what the big deal was.

She shrugged. "You could tell Jerry or one of the crew guys, and they'd tell someone and they'd tell someone, and a week from now it'll be on *TMZ*: 'Becca Cody can't read'."

She put her hands up to make brackets abound an invisible tabloid cover. She closed her eyes and shuddered like the idea was painful to her.

"You *can* read. It's okay, Becca. I bet other kids who were dyslexic would actually be like inspired or whatever if they knew."

She looked at me again as if she were considering it. Then she frowned again. "That's my call to make."

"I won't tell anyone. I swear. I'm a vault."

She stared at me a long beat, as if she was deciding whether or not to believe me.

"I don't tell a lot of people," she said quietly, her defenses down again.

I didn't bother to say that it was nothing to be ashamed of. Because she clearly didn't agree with me.

I just picked up the paper and began to read the lines again.

THIRTEEN

I loved reading scripts with Becca, but the script
department was not for me. I couldn't deal with
the copying, the collating, or the delivering.
And it kinda showed. I was late a few times.
Worse still, I messed up the page version on a
few scripts. Sarah caught it before I passed them
out, but her face told me she was freaked by the
close call.

"We can't do this stuff halfway, Jason," she
warned. "We could easily lose a whole day of
shooting with a mistake like this. Do you know
how much that would cost?"

I didn't, of course, but how much could it be? And who cared? These people were loaded.

* * *

There were a few other mistakes, and I could tell people were getting frustrated. I could see their expectations falling. Worse, some of them tried to pick up the slack—like they thought I was clearly out of my league. I hated it all. Especially when Becca saw someone correcting me or taking over some stupid job I'd messed up.

FOURTEEN

The next week, I finally moved departments. I wondered if I would see Becca. I wonder if she'd avoid me altogether.

Sam led me to the props department. "Meet Will and Adam Rice."

Same last name? Two guys, one old and one young, both wearing ball caps with a company logo, ran the department. They were a father-and-son team.

I assumed that they were like Jerry. They'd had some other Hollywood dream, but they'd chosen this one instead. But it turned out that props were the family business. The art department designed the sets, but the props department found all the items that brought that vision to life. They were responsible for the tiny things, like making sure that there was the right kind of toothbrush in the bathroom of the set, all the way up to the bigger things, like finding that vintage pinball machine that played a pivotal part in act three of the screenplay.

They had an elaborate system. Every item was logged in, and every prop for every day was on a schedule. Adam did most of the talking, and his dad looked on with a mixture of pride and approval as he showed me the color-coded system that they lived by.

There were no perks working in the props department. I could be anywhere. I barely saw the set. I never saw Becca. I spent all my time inventorying a prop cage full of junk.

I knew I wasn't, but I felt like I was being punished for something. It sucked.

I wondered how these guys did this every day, but they seemed really happy with their jobs.

FIFTEEN

When I screw up, I never do it halfway, Nina always said. And this was no different. None of this crap really mattered. It was make-believe, right?

But they all took it so very seriously.

While Will was off getting a new old pinball machine, and Adam was in accounting filling out forms for more petty cash, the phone in the prop cage rang.

"Will and Adam aren't here."

"Well, we need the vase on set ASAP."

"Well, like I said. . . ."

"Jason, I'm authorizing you to bring it," Sam said, sounding a little annoyed and under pressure at the same time.

"Fine," I said, sounding annoyed right back.

I glanced over the props for today. There were two vases. I took the larger one and headed to set.

When I got there, Sam pointed and I handed Becca the vase. She didn't smile. She was focused or preparing for something. She was making some kind of weird sound with her throat like she was trying to clear it.

Sam waved me back to the side of the set with a stop-bothering-the-actress look. I stood by his side as Brent called, "Action."

Becca was flawless once again. She managed somehow to seem scared and strong at the exact same time. It was an amazing performance, except for one thing: the vase, the one that I'd brought, was supposed to break at the end of the scene. Only instead it bounced.

Becca was staring at me, her eyes flashing with anger. I'd ruined her best take. She'd have to do it again.

"Props—what's wrong with my vase?"

I stepped forward, ready to get yelled at.

But Adam was already racing into the set carrying the right vase—actually a box of them. He was running so hard he had to hold down the baseball cap he always wore.

The vases in the box were breakaway glass. The kind that broke into a million safe pieces. The one I'd picked up was one of those plastic ones that you could never break. "He didn't know. Here's the right one."

Becca took the right vase. And closed her eyes, doing a weird breathing thing like she was trying to hold down her anger, or maybe just get back to that place she was in before my wrong vase had taken her out of it.

They had to do the take about five more times before she nailed it again.

When Adam and I were walking away, I couldn't help but ask, "Why did you cover for me?" Not that everyone didn't know I was the one who screwed up, but he'd stood up for me when he didn't have to.

"It's my department. It's my responsibility,"

Adam said without missing a beat. "But if you do it again, you should go ahead and move to the next department ahead of schedule."

"I don't see what the big deal is. Does it really matter? "

"You're right, kinda. What we do here, when it comes down to it, is make-believe. But when you take a job—any job—you treat it with respect. You do your very best out of respect for all the other people who are putting this thing together. And if you can't do that, you don't belong here."

Was he offering me an out?

Did I want out?

SIXTEEN

The next day, I showed up at her trailer at lunchtime.

But the door was locked, and she didn't answer at first. I knocked harder.

She opened the door looking mad.

"Listen, I'm sorry about the prop thing, okay. I never want to screw things up for you," I said.

"That's not the point," she said, sounding disappointed for some reason I didn't get.

"I can tell you want me to apologize."

"It's not just about me. Or me and you."

I blinked up at her, more confused than ever. Was there a string of words that I could put together to wipe that frown off her face and get us back to the place where hanging out in her trailer felt natural?

"I can't be around someone who doesn't take what I love seriously. Can't take any of this seriously. I've been working at this since I was five years old. And you walk around like it doesn't even matter. If you don't care, you shouldn't be here. And if you don't care, I can't be with you."

I opened my mouth to say something, but she cut me off.

"Movies are collaboration. It's not a one-man show. What we do here, we do as a team. And either you're on the team or you're not."

She'd really drunk the we-are-family Kool-Aid, but I hadn't. "You can't really believe that. You're a star. If you don't think that you're different, check out all the zeros on your paycheck and compare them to the script girl's."

Her look shifted from fierce to hurt.

"I have to get to set. I actually care if I'm late."

SEVENTEEN

When I got back to the hotel, Nick, Holt's assistant, was there.

I was pretty sure I was getting special treatment because of the whole foster thing. He'd brought groceries and takeout.

"Just checking in. You'll have a drop-by from child services next week. I'd like to be here for it. If possible."

I nodded and dropped my backpack on the mini couch in my room.

Nick began unpacking the groceries: lots of prepackaged meals—the fancy kind that Becca had on set to keep her flawless figure.

"Are you putting me on a diet?" I asked.

He held up one of the meals. "No, these taste way better than they look. How's it going on set?"

"It's cool."

"Really?" he asked, arching his eyebrows. He wasn't wearing business clothes this time. He was wearing a polo shirt and jeans. He looked younger and less polished somehow. I liked him better like this.

"Did they rat me out?" Did Nick actually have a contact on set? Did they give report cards? How did this work? How much did he really know about me?

"No, you just did. What's going on, Jason?"

"I don't know if I'm a good fit there."

"Why don't you just start from the beginning?" he said simply.

My voice came out flat and hard. "You can leave, man. We can skip the whole pity party. I'm good—"

"You think I pity you?" he cut in, sounding like the idea couldn't be further from the truth.

I was used to pity. The whole no-parents thing was something that I didn't think about, until I saw that look—that total poor-Jason look—written all over someone else's face. It was written on Nick's right now. Or at least I thought that was what I was looking at.

"Poor little Orphan Jason—" I said, sure that I had finally shut him up. Pulling the orphan card always worked.

Nick shook his head.

"You got a tough break. You're not the only one. I was in the system too, Jason."

My mouth opened to say something smart, but nothing came. Nick, a foster kid? I couldn't see it. And how did he get from there to being Harmon Holt's assistant?

"So you're here to show me the light or something? Let me guess, you never blew an opportunity this big."

"Oh, I blew it, but then I got a second chance and I didn't blow that. I was just as stupid as you are. And then I wasn't."

I expected him to make an exit after that. But he sat there and began unwrapping the takeout.

Nick was from where I was from. He knew that actions spoke louder than words. Right now he was saying that no matter what I threw at him, he wasn't going anywhere.

EIGHTEEN

Before he left after dinner, Nick did leave one last piece of advice.

"You don't have to buy into the whole team thing, kid. But that doesn't mean that you can't learn everything you can from that place. Make a good impression. Get something out of it for you."

"They've pretty much made up their minds about me."

"Then unmake them. It's a long summer."

* * *

The next day on set I'd moved departments again, but I was searching for a way to move Becca. At lunch, after spending hours answering calls in the production office, I knocked on her trailer door. It opened, but she wasn't there. I wasn't a grand-gesture guy. But I knew I had to do something, or when the shoot was over I would never talk to or see Becca again. That would probably happen anyway.

NINETEEN

"Hey, stranger." Nina had picked up on the first ring. "You okay?"

I sighed into the phone.

"Jason," she demanded. She could tell within five seconds if I was in trouble or not, so I might as well just spill everything already. No point in sugarcoating anything.

"I screwed up a couple of times on set. I met Becca Cody, but now she thinks I'm a clown. How do I make her see that I'm really sorry? That I'm serious?"

When I was little, I'd wanted Nina to adopt

me. But she had thirty other kids to check on. She couldn't adopt every single one. Even when I was little I understood that. She was still the closest thing to family that I'd ever had.

She saw through my crap, and she never judged me.

There was a long silence on the other end of the phone.

"Do the hard stuff. Show up on time. Be helpful and don't complain. She'll come back to you when she can see that you're trying."

"Couldn't I just make her a video or something?"

"You can do that, too. But you have to do the other stuff to back it up. Otherwise your grand gesture is an empty one."

I nodded, even though I knew she couldn't see me.

"So, is she as pretty as she looks on-screen?" Nina asked, sounding more like a schoolgirl than my social worker.

"Prettier."

A few minutes later, after confirming that I was eating and sleeping and whatever, we hung up. I looked at the brand-new camera that I hadn't actually shot anything on yet, but I didn't pick it up. Instead, I kicked off my shoes and climbed into bed.

TWENTY

I'd heard what Nina had said, but the idea of making the video had already taken hold. I had a day off, and I was going to use it to make a video to make it up to her.

I was used to working with clay subjects. Real people were harder. But I had to do something major.

I found the cheerleading girl I'd met on day one and a couple of the other kids from the acting class. It was a start.

The cheerleader's name was Tamara. She wanted to know where the script was. I didn't have one, but I didn't let that stop me. We just sort of wrote one as we went. It was mostly me hamming it up, trying to apologize without actually saying I was sorry. Just when my character became too much, Tamara cartwheeled in and did this stupid football cheer/apology thing she'd made up on the spot. It was cheesy, but I hoped it was cult-following cheesy instead of walk-out-of-the-theater cheesy. Anyway, it was the best shot I had.

When we were done, Tamara helped me pack up my camera, and she told me a little about her Hollywood dreams. Because of course she had Hollywood dreams. Everyone here did. She was a triple threat—singer/dancer/actress—but no one seemed to know it yet. Her family let her come out to LA every summer for auditions. She had been doing it since she was six. She'd gotten a couple of commercials and had little parts in two pilots, but that was it. Still, she had the dream. And the discipline.

I walked Tamara back to her room, and even though I promised to send her the video,

I thought maybe she still was holding out for more. Or maybe I was just full of myself.

TWENTY-ONE

I texted Becca a link to my video and waited for a response. Nothing.

In the morning. I still hadn't heard from her. At lunchtime, she finally texted, and I went to her trailer.

"No one's ever apologized to me by video before," she said. It wasn't a compliment. But I was standing in her trailer again. That had to be progress. "I looked up your videos on YouTube. Really cool. My first work was so embarrassing. But yours . . . you have nothing to be embarrassed about."

"Thanks," I said, but I meant a lot more. Having a real actress like my work felt like a big deal. "So your first work was embarrassing, huh? How embarrassing? What was it? Diaper commercial?"

"No, cereal. I must have eaten like hundred bowls of that crap—and there was really big hair and missing teeth and . . . wait for it . . . there was dancing."

"I'd think you'd be an amazing dancer."

"You'd think wrong. I don't think that they even aired it. It was that bad."

"I bet you still looked great. You always do."

She looked at me a long beat as if she were considering liking me again. Then she picked up the script. She held tight to it as if to remind me and herself that she was all business.

"I should leave you to it," I said, hoping she'd ask me to stay.

"I think your work is good, but if you used a script it would be that much better."

"What?" Was she actually critiquing my apology video? I felt myself getting defensive.

"There are directors who do the whole

improv thing, but I think you have to know how to do it from a script first."

I blurted. "Are you actually giving me notes on my gift? What about a thank-you? If you don't like it—"

"That's not what I said. Jason, if you could just listen . . ."

I was done listening. I stood up. I headed for her door.

TWENTY-TWO

I could hear Becca's footsteps behind me.

"Don't do this," she said when I got to the door.

I paused with my hand on the doorknob.

Then I pushed through. I blinked. It took a second for my eyes to adjust to the light. I was surprised to see that she followed me all the way out of the trailer.

"Don't walk away. I never took you as the drama queen type," she said.

I saw what she was doing. I just didn't understand why. I leaned against the trailer wall.

"There's only room for one diva on this set, and I think it should be me," she continued.

I didn't say anything, but I didn't move either. It was hard not to smirk, though. There was no diva in her.

"Why do you care what I do?"

She paused and bit her lip, like she had to think about it.

"I don't know. Maybe because I need someone to help me with my scripts."

I peeled myself off the wall, preparing to go. She stopped me with one hand in the center of my chest. I couldn't move. Or at least I didn't want to anymore.

"Jason, you're the first person I've met who doesn't get the magic of this place. You can't leave before you get to the good part."

I could barely breathe with her touching me. But I didn't want her to know that. I took a step back. "What's the good part?"

"For me, it's when I'm in front of the camera. For you, I guess it'll be somewhere between right now and when you shoot your first real film."

"So how many cups of coffee and scripts and props do I have to deliver before I get there? It doesn't sound like fun."

"A lot, probably. You're seventeen, and you just got started."

"You're younger than me."

"And I started when I was three. I didn't get my big break until two years ago. You do the math."

"Well, I can't wait ten years, Becca."

"Maybe you won't have to. But you have to want it badly enough. And you have to learn to enjoy even the crappy jobs because they're a step in the direction of what you really want."

"And what if I can't?"

"Then you should keep on walking. But I hope you stick around." With that she slipped back inside her trailer.

TWENTY-THREE

I didn't go back. I went home.

On the way, I called Nina.

I didn't usually talk about my love life with Nina—but I made an exception because she was the person I went to when I really didn't know what to do.

I told her what happened.

Nina sighed heavily, like I exhausted her somehow. "Jason, you screw things up before anything good can happen. I've seen you do it with classes, with families, even with friends. You get anywhere close to something good and you start trying to figure out a way to blow it—"

"That's not true—" But even as I said it, I could still feel her words thudding around in my head like an echo or something.

"But it doesn't have to be," she said sternly. Then, gentler, she added, "When you made those videos for that class, it was the first time you saw something all the way through. And look what happened. You're in L.A. On a sound-stage. You killed it. You can do it again, if you let yourself."

"She's a movie star, Nina."

"She's still a girl—and I bet with all the crap she has to deal with out there, she's overdue to have a dose of something real. Someone real."

TWENTY-FOUR

When I got home, Nick was there for the child services visit. The social worker showed up right after I did. Mrs. Hayden wasn't anything like Nina. She was older and more businesslike. But she was fast. I answered all the questions before she could ask them. Was I happy? Was I comfortable? Did I miss home? (That was the kicker. I couldn't miss something I hadn't had.)

After she left, I told Nick about what Becca said.

"She's not wrong," Nick said simply. "Think about it. What is everything you're seeing at work telling you? It's a process. Writing it instead of winging it makes sense to me."

"But what if I liked my videos? They made people laugh. Even Harmon Holt liked them. It was good work." Something twisted in my gut. It felt like he was trying to tear down the one thing I had that belonged to me.

"It was good. But that doesn't mean that your next project can't be even better. It is okay to grow, Jason. You can't stand still forever, kid."

I didn't answer. He let the words sink in for a beat before he shifted the subject to sports. He floated the idea of taking me to a Lakers game. "Harmon has seats that he doesn't use."

I didn't bother hiding my excitement about Lakers seats. I hadn't been outside of the apartments or the studio in weeks. I felt a smile creep across my face. I remembered I was mad at him for what he'd said about my work, but could I really let that keep me from my first Lakers game?

TWENTY-FIVE

The next morning, I knocked on Tamara's door. I didn't know what I was doing there. To thank her. To ask her out. It probably wasn't a good idea, since my brain was still stuck on Becca. Even if she probably wanted nothing to do with me now.

A girl I'd never met before answered.

"Hey, is Tamara around?"

"Oh, you mean the girl who was here before. She went back to Detroit. She says she'll be back for pilot season." The girl closed the door in my face.

Tamara had left without saying good-bye.

I knew that this was how the business worked. But Tamara had tried and failed and would come back and try again.

I went back to my room and ticked off the hours until Nick took me to the game.

* * *

The Lakers game was awesome. We had seats that were so close to the players that I could see the sweat drip off Kobe.

For a couple of hours I forgot about Becca and the business and all of it.

When we walked out of the arena, it all came crushing back. I tried to push it aside.

When I got back, there was a laptop on my desk with a note: "Write something." It was on the blue Harmon Holt stationery, but Nick had signed it.

I pushed the computer away from me and went to the fridge to make dinner.

A few minutes later I opened the laptop and began writing.

When I was done, I sent the script to Becca.

TWENTY-SIX

When I saw Becca the next day, she gave me a half-smile and told me to meet her at her trailer at lunch. I was sure that all was forgiven. But I didn't exactly know how—she couldn't have noticed after one day that I was on time and not complaining, could she?

When I got there, she handed her script to me. It was a green day, and there were lots of green pages. Lots of lines to learn.

"I thought you wanted nothing to do with me," I said.

"Just because we're in a fight doesn't mean

that my work should suffer."

I tried to follow her logic. But I wasn't quite there yet. I wasn't sure if it was that I didn't understand girls or movie stars.

* * *

But the script alone didn't do it. Just like the video hadn't. Nina had been right all along. It took weeks. Weeks of showing up on time and not screwing up. Weeks of actually getting to know the other people and taking things seriously that I never thought I'd do. Organizing wardrobe, shredding scripts, getting coffee, everything.

And one day, in the middle of day, while we were reading lines, she squeezed my hand even though nothing in the script called for it.

TWENTY-SEVEN

A few days later we were reading again. There weren't many lines—just a lot of screaming—so Becca suggested that we play a game. She called it *Truth or Scare*. Tell the truth or do something that scared you.

I agreed. Not because I wanted to play, but because it meant that Becca had maybe started to forgive me.

"My real name isn't Becca. It's Bridget. But since there was another Bridget Cody, I had to change mine. Your turn."

"I don't think that your name reveal counts

for truth or scare. It's not exactly deep or dark, and I bet I could have found that on the Internet."

"I bet that you could find out most things about me on the Internet. But I can't exactly google you."

"You want to hear my deep, dark secrets?"

She nodded.

"Why?"

"I want to know where all that attitude comes from."

"Perfect home. Mom's a teacher. Dad too. We live in a perfect two-story house in the suburbs," I lied. I didn't want her pity.

"You family sounds perfect. Mine, not so much. Dad was never in the picture, so it was just me and my mom. So when she lost her job, she said we could give the whole L.A. thing a shot. I've been making our living ever since. Mom's my manager. There were some really lean times the first few years. But after a while I started getting more commercial work. Then a soap opera, then *New York Horror Story*. Then, once I made a little money, my dad showed up.

He demanded money or he'd start talking to the press about us. We paid him off. And we lived happily ever after. I hope."

I didn't read the tabloids, but I didn't think that I'd ever heard anything about her having a deadbeat dad. I felt something in my gut like a punch from Trig. It was guilt. She'd shared a piece of herself, and I'd lied.

"My family isn't really perfect. I made all that stuff up."

She didn't even blink. "I know. You're a terrible actor."

I told her about foster care. About Nina. About Trig. About Stella. For a split second I saw the pity look—but she wiped it away just as quickly. Like she knew that it wasn't what I needed. Like she got that it was enough that I told her. She didn't have to go to mush about it.

She switched the subject back to her. She didn't go to regular school. Her education was a lot different than mine. It prepared her for the same standardized tests that all kids have to take, but other than that she got to learn what she wanted. "When I was little I was obsessed with the Greek myths. Those stories were so crazy, so far out there. I ate them up. There's this one where a guy, his name was Sisyphus, had to push a boulder up a mountain every day. And every it would roll back down again. And every day he would push it back up again."

"Acting is like that?"

"No, the business side is. You're always pushing your way uphill. Only to have it push you back down again."

"And you do that voluntarily." I'd been pushed down my whole life. But I never asked for it.

"Because when I'm actually acting, it's the best feeling in the world." She looked far away, as if she was remembering how good it felt.

"And it's worth it?"

"Yeah, it's worth it."

The rock had flattened Tamara. At least for the season. Would it finish me, too? The shooting schedule was on its last pages. I'd find out soon enough, I guess.

TWENTY-EIGHT

The wrap party was at a club downtown. It had a bouncer at the door, and a girl with a clipboard and a list checked off my name before the bouncer lifted the velvet rope. When I got inside I saw the whole crew looking like different people. Gone were the Converse and the hoodies. Guys were wearing button-down shirts, and girls were dressed up in sparkly tops and jeans.

Becca, who always looked good, looked even better. Her hair was down. She was wearing a tiny dress that grazed all the right parts. Her eyes met mine, and she smiled a little brighter, like she was smiling for me.

I noticed Brent in the corner, holding court. I thought about introducing myself. But he hadn't said a word to me in the two months I'd been here. What would I say? Would he remember me as that guy who screwed up that time?

Becca suddenly appeared next to me. She gave me a kiss on the cheek. In public. The question that had been nagging at me since the moment I thought maybe we were something pricked at me again. She was a movie star, and I was a nobody. We had a pretty clear expiration date, and the clock was ticking right now. Tonight might just be it for us. If there was an us at all.

"You should go talk to him."

I shook my head. "What would I say?"

"I could introduce you?"

I shook my head again. I couldn't have Brent Tollin thinking I couldn't walk up to him on my own.

"Or not," she said and pulled me back into the crowd. We talked to the all the other crew people that I'd met from other departments.

Jerry actually got on the dance floor. He could move. I laughed out loud. But Becca didn't just laugh. She went out on the dance floor and joined him. Once Becca hit the dance floor, more of the crew joined her. She waved at me to come and join her, but I shook my head again and went back to the bar. Brent was standing next to it.

Now or never. "Hi, I'm Jason. I've been interning this summer. It's a real honor to see how you do what you do."

He looked at me for a moment. "You were the guy who cost me my best take."

"Sorry about that."

"But I'm told that you're also one of the hardest-working people on the set."

He'd heard about me. From who?

"Thank you," was all I could say. Then he tilted his beer at me and headed back to a circle of crew members.

Becca appeared again. "Come outside with me. I have to tell you something," she whispered in my ear.

TWENTY-NINE

By the time we got out to the terrace, I'd decided that she'd brought me out to say good-bye. I paced away from her.

"Jason—" she said softly. I would miss her saying my name.

"Becca," I cut her off. "We both know what this is and what this isn't." I said it simply, proud of my choice of words even though they stung me as I said them.

Her face clouded over. "Do we?" She was going to make me say it.

"It was summer. And now it's over. Isn't that

what you were going to say?"

She shook her head slowly like I was a stupid little kid. "I took a new movie. It's called *The DOP.*"

"Good for you. What does DOP stand for?" I said, trying to make small talk. Trying to sound like we were just friends. That I was cool. That appreciated the time that we'd had, but I was ready to pretend like nothing happened. She got a brand-new movie and put me in her rearview. And what did I get? A few memories that I would live over and over again.

"Daughter of the president. It shoots in DC. I start next month."

"Wait—DC?" I drifted off.

She smiled again. And then she leaned in, and she kissed me. I'd kissed girls before. But no one that I'd liked this much. Her lips were sticky and soft from the gloss. They tasted like some kind of exotic fruit that I'd never had before. When we broke, I felt dizzy for a second. I opened my eyes and looked at her to see if she was as affected by the kiss as I was. She exhaled deeply and squeezed my hand.

"We should get back."

"Just a minute longer."

She nodded, and I looked out at the view before I kissed her again.

THIRTY

Before we walked inside she said, "I want to do it."

"What exactly?" I asked.

"Your screenplay. Your short film. I read it—and I want to do it. And everyone else does, too."

"You what?"

"I gave copies to Minnie and the prop guys and Sam. We're all in. We could shoot it in an afternoon. It could be great."

"You're not serious."

But she was.

"If we plan it right we can do this."

I nodded. I got the whole planning thing now. The teamwork thing. I got how all the pieces and people had to work together to pull it off. And I was ready to do it myself. With a little—well, a lot—of help from my friends.

The next day—my last day in L.A.—we shot a little movie. My movie.

THIRTY-ONE

Nick picked me up at the Oakland.

He didn't do the whole I-told-you-so thing, even though I deserved it. He just watched my new movie and gave me props for it. It was just a horror short, but he said it showed real promise. I managed to thank him.

I was nervous about going back to my normal life. I didn't want to go back to living at Stella's and back to school. But at least I had things to look forward to.

Somehow Nick sensed what was up with me, or maybe it was just written all over my face as we pulled away from the place I'd spent my summer. "Hey, it's tough going back to the real world. But once the door's open even a crack, you keep pushing right on through." Nick was kind of a mind reader. No wonder he'd done so well.

"There's no map for this career that you've chosen. You can keep working on sets. And there are lots of college programs, but it's not like banking or being a lawyer. Some people never break in. Others end up taking crazy detours."

I thought of Jerry. "So you think I should pick something safer?"

"No way. No one's better prepared for a career like this."

"How do you figure that?"

"You've never had safe. You don't know what you're missing." He smiled when he said it, but he looked far away, as if he was maybe remembering his own rise.

When I got on the plane, I had texts from Nina, Becca, and even Brent. I still didn't have a home exactly. But maybe home wasn't a place exactly. Maybe for me it was a list like this.

People I could call when I screwed up. People I could call when I was on top of the world.

Dear Mr. Holt,

Thank you for the opportunity. I went into this whole experience with maybe not the best attitude. In fact, I went into this thing not expecting much. But I was wrong. I didn't think I belonged on a film set. And once I got there, I thought I was too good for all the small-time stuff that happens on set. But I get it now. The small-time stuff, from props to craft services, is all part of moviemaking, and without it the big-time stuff couldn't be possible. And I want to be big-time. I'm willing to do what it takes to get there.

Sincerely,
Jason Hart

ABOUT THE AUTHOR

D. M. Paige attended Columbia University and her first internship eventually led her to her first writing job at *Guiding Light*, a soap opera. She writes and lives in New York City.

IT'S THE OPPORTUNITY OF A LIFETIME— IF YOU CAN HANDLE IT.

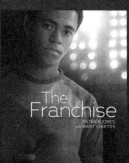

THE OPPORTUNITY

SOUTHSIDE HIGH

ARE YOU A SURVIVOR?

 THE Alliance

 BAD DEAL

 BEATEN

 BENITO RUNS

 DANCE TEAM

 DEADLY DRIVE

 THE FIGHT

 FULL IMPACT

 OVEREXPOSED

 PLAN B

 RECRUITED

 SHATTERED STAR

Check out all the books in the

SURVIVING · SOUTH SIDE

collection

WELCOME TO THE DOJO

LEARN TO FIGHT,
LEARN TO LIVE,
AND LEARN
TO FIGHT
FOR YOUR
LIFE.

TRAVEL TEAM
THE CATCH

TRAVEL TEAM
FORCED OUT

TRAVEL TEAM
HIGH HEAT

TRAVEL TEAM
OUT OF CONTROL

TRAVEL TEAM
POWER HITTER

TRAVEL TEAM
THE PROSPECT